THE LITTLE HOUSE ON STILTS

AND OTHER STORIES

ILLUSTRATED BY LUCIA PATTON

WRITTEN BY

LUCIA PATTON

AND

MARGARET FRISKEY

The Little House on Stilts
Written and illustrated by Lucia Patton
First published in 1948

The Little River of Gold
Written and illustrated by Lucia Patton
First published in 1946

Randy and the Crimson Rocket
Written by Margaret Friskey
Illustrated by Lucia Patton
First published in 1944

Cover illustration by Nada Serafimovic
Cover design by Tina DeKam
This unabridged version has updated grammar and spelling.
© 2019 Jenny Phillips
www.thegoodandthebeautiful.com

TABLE OF CONTENTS

THE LITTLE
HOUSE
ON STILTS

STORY AND PICTURES BY LUCIA PATTON

To my partners
my mother and father
and my husband

Mother was making cookies. Johnny and Judy were watching her.

"They look good," said Johnny.

"They smell good," said Judy.

"Maybe they taste good," said Mother. "Try some."

"Um-m—they are good!" said Johnny and Judy.

"May we take some to Mrs. Lee at the Lookout Tower?" asked Judy.

"Yes," said Mother, "and tell her that we are glad that she and Mr. Lee are here for the summer."

Mother put some cookies in a bag. Johnny and Judy put the saddles on their little donkeys.

The little donkeys trotted down the road with Johnny and Judy.

"I would like to be a Forest Ranger like Mr. Lee," said Johnny.

"I would like to live in the little house on the Lookout Tower," said Judy.

The little donkeys were walking slowly up the steep path to the tower.

"Look," said Johnny, "I see the little house."

"It looks like a little house on stilts," said Judy.

"Here comes Pete," said Johnny. Pete was Mr. Lee's dog.

"Bow wow! Bow wow!" barked Pete.

"Hi, Pete," said Johnny.

"He is telling Mr. and Mrs. Lee that we are coming," said Judy.

"He was a war dog with Mr. Lee in the Marines," said Johnny.

"Yes," said Judy. "He carried important messages for Mr. Lee."

Johnny and Judy came up to the Lookout Tower.

"Hi, Johnny and Judy!" said Mr. Lee.

"Hello, Johnny and Judy!" called Mrs. Lee from the door of the little house on stilts.

"We brought you some of Mother's fresh cookies," said Judy.

"How nice!" said Mrs. Lee. "Come up."

Johnny and Judy climbed the steps of the tower.

"Oh, my!" said Judy. "We can see all over the world up here."

"Well," said Mr. Lee, "at least we can see all over this part of the National Forest. But Little Squaw Mountain hides the beautiful pine forest down by the old mill. This makes one bad blind spot."

"Look through these field glasses," said Mrs. Lee. "You can see just the red roof of the old mill."

"Oh!" said Johnny. "It looks close through these."

"Do you look out all the time?" asked Judy.

"We are on guard here all summer," said Mr. Lee. "When the weather is hot and the forest is dry, we watch for fires harder than ever."

"In a few hours, a fire can burn down a forest that took many years to grow," said Mrs. Lee.

"How do fires start?" asked Johnny.

"Sometimes lightning strikes a dry tree," said Mr. Lee. "But most fires start because people are careless. You can be Junior Forest Rangers by watching for fires."

"We will!" said Johnny.

"Good!" said Mr. Lee. "Guarding the forest is an important job."

"We must ride home now," said Judy. "Mother said to come right back."

"Goodbye, and thank you for the cookies," said Mrs. Lee.

"Come again," said Mr. Lee.

Pete barked as Johnny and Judy rode away.

One day Johnny and Judy were riding their little donkeys through the beautiful pine forest down by the old mill.

"I can't see the Lookout Tower from here," said Judy.

"No," said Johnny. "This is Little Squaw Mountain. This is the blind spot that Mr. Lee told us about."

An owl flew past them.

"Hey," said Judy. "Where is that old fellow going? He should be asleep. Owls don't fly in the daytime."

A blue jay flew past. Four robins and six sparrows flew past.

"They must be having a parade," said Johnny.

A ground squirrel ran by, then three rabbits and a chipmunk.

"Johnny!" said Judy. "I smell smoke!"

"I do, too!" said Johnny. "Maybe that is why all the animals are running away."

"Look!" cried Judy.

Under the pine trees they could see bright flames. A low fire was burning the pine needles on the ground.

"Maybe we can put it out," said Johnny.

"No," said Judy. "We have no water and we have no shovels to cover it with dirt. We must tell Mr. Lee quickly!"

"That's right," said Johnny. "It is getting too big for us to put out. Hurry!"

Judy and Johnny turned the little donkeys around. They rode as fast as they could. They rode up the steep path to the Lookout Tower.

"Fire! Fire! Mr. Lee!" they called.

"Hello!" said Mr. Lee. "Are you playing a joke on me?"

"No!" cried Johnny. "There is a fire down by the road to the old mill."

"It is in that bad blind spot," said Mr. Lee. "I will telephone the Forest Ranger Headquarters. Then I will try to put out the fire."

Mr. Lee ran up the steps of the tower. Johnny and Judy followed him.

Mrs. Lee opened the door. "What is the trouble?" she asked.

"There may be real trouble," said Mr. Lee. "Johnny and Judy saw a fire down by the old mill behind Little Squaw Mountain."

Mr. Lee telephoned Forest Ranger
Headquarters. Then he said, "Johnny and
Judy, you stay here until the trouble is over.
Pete and I will find the fire. If I need help, I
will send the message to you in the bag on
Pete's collar. Pete is a good messenger."

Mrs. Lee said, "We will call your mother, Johnny and Judy. We will ask her to tell the neighbors to be ready to help."

Mr. Lee tied an ax and a shovel to the
saddle on his horse. He tied a water bag to
Pete's back.

"Be good soldiers," he called. "You are on guard here."

He rode off on his big brown horse. Pete ran along beside him.

Mrs. Lee telephoned Mother. Johnny
and Judy looked out toward Little Squaw
Mountain.

"I don't see any smoke," said Johnny.

"No," said Judy. "Little Squaw Mountain
is in the way."

Mrs. Lee looked through the field glasses.
"Oh look, Judy," she said. "There is smoke
now over the edge of Little Squaw."

Judy looked through the glasses. "I see flames," she said.

"I'd like to be down there," said Johnny.

"No," said Mrs. Lee. "We are on guard here."

In a few minutes, they heard Pete bark. He came running up the path. Johnny and Judy and Mrs. Lee ran down the tower steps. They found the note in the bag on Pete's collar.

"Fire spreading north. Call Headquarters for help. Fill Pete's water bag and send him back to me."

Mrs. Lee went to the tower. She called the Forest Ranger Headquarters. Judy filled Pete's water bag. Pete stood still while Johnny tied the bag on his back.

"Go to your master," said Johnny. "Good dog. Go!"

Pete ran off down the path.

Johnny and Judy knew that he would find his master. They went back up into the tower.

Mrs. Lee said, "Forest Ranger Head-quarters will send help."

From the big windows, Johnny and Judy
could see flames moving like a big snake
around Little Squaw. Through the field
glasses, they could see men running. The men
were chopping down trees ahead of the fire.

"They are cutting a wide path where there will be nothing to burn," said Mrs. Lee.

After a long, long time, the red flames could not be seen. There were only puffs of smoke. The fire was out. The men were resting.

At last they heard Pete bark. They saw Mr. Lee riding up the path. Mother and Father were riding with him.

"The fire is out," he called. "Hurrah for the heroes!"

"What heroes?" asked Johnny and Judy.

"You. Both of you," said Mr. Lee. "By using your eyes, you found the fire. By using your heads, you came to the right place for help. The pine forest and the old mill are safe. You are real Junior Forest Rangers now. Here are your badges."

"Oh, boy! Thanks!" said Johnny.

"Thank you," said Judy.

"Three cheers for Johnny and Judy!" said Mother and Father and Mr. and Mrs. Lee. Pete barked and barked and barked.

Mother and Father and Johnny and
Judy rode down the path. They looked
back at the little house on stilts and waved
goodbye. They all rode home through the
pine forest.

"Look, Johnny and Judy," said Father. "These beautiful tall pine trees are alive because of you."

"Listen," said Mother. "The wind in their branches is saying thank you."

Johnny and Judy looked up into the high branches. They listened. They were very happy.

A fat robin chirped nearby. A brown squirrel sat on a log and chattered. Johnny laughed and said, "Listen. They are saying thank you, too."

"That's right," said Judy. "I think they are messengers for all the forest creatures saying thank you for saving our homes."

THE LITTLE RIVER OF GOLD

STORY AND PICTURES BY LUCIA PATTON

To my mother and father,
who see love and beauty
in all things

Johnny and Judy were watching the rain.

"Judy," said Johnny, "see the rainbow?
Father says there is a pot of gold at the foot
of every rainbow."

"I wish we could find the pot of gold," said Judy.

"Mother," said Johnny, "may we ride to find the pot of gold? It has stopped raining."

"You may ride as far as the old mill," said Mother.

Johnny had a little donkey named Mike.

Judy had a little donkey named Joe.

Johnny climbed on Mike.

Judy climbed on Joe.

They rode up-up-up to the top of the
mountain.

"Oh, Judy," said Johnny, "we can see both
ends of the rainbow. How beautiful!"

"How big it is!" said Judy. "One end is in the cornfield. The other end is near that pine tree down in the valley."

"Yes," said Johnny, "it is on the road to the old mill. Let's go and find that pot of gold. Giddyup, Mike!"

Both little donkeys went trot-trot-trot
down the road. The road went into the
beautiful pine forest.

Suddenly, both little donkeys stopped.

They did not eat the grass.

They did not move.

"Well!" said Johnny. "Why don't you go?"

Johnny got off and pulled Mike.

Judy got off and pushed Joe.

Both little donkeys stood still.

"Johnny," said Judy, "I think Mike and Joe are afraid. Let's get back on."

"No," said Johnny. "What is there to be afraid of? Sometimes animals know more about the forest than we do. Let's listen."

They climbed back on the donkeys.

They sat still.

It was very quiet.

The wind in the pine trees blew softly.

All of a sudden—Snap! Crash!

Across the trail jumped a mountain bobcat.

"Yip-ee!" cried Johnny. "He went fast."

Both the little donkeys started on the
run down the trail to the old mill. Judy and
Johnny hung on.

"Boy!" shouted Johnny, "I'm glad animals
know when to be careful!"

Near the bottom of the mountain, the little donkeys slowed down.

"We must be in the valley now," said Judy.

"Yes," said Johnny. "The foot of the rainbow was near one of these pine trees."

"Look!" cried Judy.

Under a tall pine tree, there really was something!

It was an old man.

He was down by the creek.

"Hello," said Johnny. "Did you see a pot of gold around here?"

"Hello," said the old man. "Pot of gold, did you say? Did you lose one?"

"No," said Johnny. "We were just looking for one."

"The one at the foot of the rainbow," said Judy. "We thought it was near one of these pine trees."

"Well, you are just about right," said the old man. "Only this creek is better than a pot of gold. This creek is a river of gold. Watch now."

The old man took a flat pan.

He dipped some sand and water from the creek into it.

He shook the pan from side to side. Then he poured off the water and the sand. There were some bright, shining grains left in the bottom of the pan.

"Is that gold?" asked Johnny.

"Yes," said the old man, "as sure as I am called Uncle Tom. Here, you try it."

He gave a pan to Johnny. He gave a pan to Judy.

Johnny dipped up a panful. Judy dipped up a panful. They shook the pans. They poured away the water.

In the bottom of the pans were more bright, shining grains.

"There is your gold!" said Uncle Tom. He poured the gold into little bags.

"Is there enough gold in this little river for all of us?" asked Judy.

"Yes," said Uncle Tom. "There is gold for all who work for it."

"Was there gold at the other end of the rainbow, too?" asked Johnny.

"It was in the cornfield," said Judy.

"Yes," said Uncle Tom, "there is gold in that cornfield. Golden corn. It is there because the farmer works to make it grow. I think God puts a rainbow in the sky as a promise to us. But He wants us to work for the gold."

Johnny and Judy and Uncle Tom worked all afternoon.

Johnny filled a little bag with gold.

Judy filled a little bag with gold.

Uncle Tom filled a little bag with gold.

Uncle Tom said, "It is time to go home. Take your little bags of gold to the Mint in Denver. There they will give you money for the gold."

"Then we can buy new shoes for Johnny and a new dress for me to wear to school," said Judy.

"Good," said Uncle Tom. "Will you ride back here to show me your new clothes?"

"Yes!" said Johnny. "We will."

They rode home as fast as Mike and Joe could go.

"Mother!" they called. "See our little bags of gold!"

"My!" said Mother. "Where did you get them?"

Johnny and Judy told Mother about Uncle Tom and the river of gold.

The next day they drove with Father and
Mother to the Mint in Denver.

The man at the Mint gave Judy and Johnny some money for their gold.

"Is it enough for shoes for Johnny and a dress for me?" asked Judy.

"Yes," said Father, "and with some left over."

"Goody," said Johnny. "We can buy a present for Uncle Tom."

They bought shoes for Johnny, a dress
for Judy, and a bright new necktie for Uncle
Tom. The necktie had stripes of color.
"It is like the rainbow," said Judy.

When they got home, Johnny put on his new shoes. Judy put on her new dress.

They rode Mike and Joe up the mountain and down the mountain and through the beautiful pine forest. They found Uncle Tom by the river of gold.

"Hello," said Uncle Tom. "What a beautiful dress you have, Judy. What nice shoes you are wearing, Johnny!"

"Here is a present for you," said Judy.

Uncle Tom opened his present. He saw the new necktie.

"Why," he said, "this is just like the rainbow that brought me two good friends, Johnny and Judy!"

"It is to say thank you," said Johnny. "It is fun to work for real gold."

"Yes," said Judy. "It is fun to hunt for rainbow gold, too."

THE END

Randy and the Crimson Rocket

by Margaret Friskey

Illustrated by Lucia Patton

Randy was playing with his electric train.

He had an engine.

He had a coal car.

He had three freight cars.

Sue was not playing with him today.

Sue was his sister.

Randy stopped his train.

He stopped his train and listened.

He heard a real train whistle.

It was the slow freight train.

The slow freight train was his friend.

Randy ran to the barn as fast as he could go.

Sue was in the barn feeding two baby lambs.

Ginger was in the barn, too.

Ginger was Randy's pony.

"Come on, Ginger!" said Randy. "Come on, or we will be late."

"I cannot go today," said Sue. "I must take care of the lambs."

Sometimes Randy rode Ginger to school.

Sometimes he rode him to town.

Ginger was a good pony.

Randy rode him well.

Best of all, Randy liked to ride Ginger across the field to see the slow freight go by.

Randy jumped on Ginger's back.

Off they went across the field.

The slow freight was coming
around the bend.

Randy waved his hand.

Old Jim waved back from the engine window.

Old Jim was the engineer.

Newt waved, too.

Newt was the fireman.

The little engine puffed and smoked.

It pulled its heavy load around the bend.

The slow freight came along the field.

The little black engine stopped.

The coal car stopped.

All the freight cars stopped, too.

"What is the matter?" asked Randy.

"Not a thing," said Old Jim.

"Have you nothing to take to the city?" asked Randy.

"I have cows and corn and cars of coal," said Old Jim.

"Then why are you stopping here?" asked Randy.

"I am waiting for something," said Old Jim. "Get up in my engine, and you will see."

Randy got off Ginger.

He climbed the fence.

He climbed into the engine.

This was the first time he had seen the inside of a real engine.

"Do you know what makes the engine go?" asked Old Jim.

"You do," said Randy.

"Oh no," said Old Jim. "Newt uses coal to make a fire. The fire heats the water. The water makes steam. The steam makes the engine go."

Old Jim showed Randy how to run a real engine.

"What are you waiting for?" asked Randy.

"I am waiting for the Crimson Rocket," said Old Jim.

"What is that?"

"That is the new fast train. It will

come by here for the first time today.
An old freight has to get out of the
way," said Old Jim.

"It is a good old freight," said Randy.

"I must pull off on the sidetrack every
day," said Old Jim.

Randy and Old Jim and Newt heard a low roar.

"There she comes!" cried Old Jim.

Around the bend came the Crimson Rocket.

The train looked like a crimson snake with a red head.

It had one big eye in the middle of its forehead.

"Swi-ish-sh-sh!" went the Crimson Rocket.

"Boy!" said Randy.

Then the Crimson Rocket was gone.

So was Ginger.

Ginger did not like the new fast train.

He ran for the barn as fast as he could go.

Newt put some coal on the fire.

"Now I can take my load to the city," said Old Jim.

"Goodbye," said Randy. He climbed out of the engine and walked toward home.

Every day Randy rode over to see the slow freight.

Every day Old Jim pulled off on the sidetrack.

Every day the Crimson Rocket went "Swi-ish-sh-sh!"

Every day Ginger ran for the barn.

Every day Randy walked back to the barn. And there was Sue feeding her lambs.

One day it was raining hard.

Randy was playing with his little train.

It was raining too hard for Randy to ride over to see the slow freight.

He listened for the whistle. Old Jim was late.

Then Randy heard it. Toot-toot-toot. Toot-toot-toot.

Randy jumped up. The slow freight must be in trouble.

Randy put on his raincoat and rubber boots and hat.

He ran to the barn.

He rode Ginger across the field as fast as he could go.

The slow freight was not in sight.

It was not on the sidetrack.

It was not even coming around the bend.

Toot-toot-toot. Toot-toot-toot.

Randy rode Ginger toward the bend.

They went around the bend.

There was the slow freight. The last car was off the track.

"What are you going to do?" asked Randy. "You cannot get out of the way of the Crimson Rocket."

"I sent a man back to flag the Rocket," said Old Jim.

"Will the engineer see him in this rain?"

"Oh, yes," said Old Jim.

Ginger stamped his feet. He wanted to go for a run.

"How fast can your pony go?" asked Old Jim.

"He can run like the wind."

"Take this lantern," said Old Jim.

"Ride along the track.

"When you see the Crimson Rocket coming, wave the lantern. That will give the Rocket more time to stop."

Randy took the lantern.

He rode as fast as he could go.

He went to the end of the field.

He rode down the road beside the track.

Ginger slipped on the mud, but he
kept going.

Soon Randy heard the low roar of the Crimson Rocket.

Then, through the rain, he saw the big eye in the middle of the forehead.

Randy waved the lantern as hard as he could.

"Swi-ish-sh-sh!" The train passed
him, then slowed down and stopped.
Ginger stood up on his hind legs.
"Quiet!" said Randy to his pony.

In one car, Randy could see people eating their supper at little tables.

He rode up to the engine.

Ginger was dancing around on his four feet.

"Quiet!" said Randy. He climbed off the pony.

The engineer was way up in the nose
of the train.

He stuck his head out of the window.

"Say! What is going on here?" he yelled.

Randy told him about the slow freight.

"It cannot get out of your way," said
Randy. "And I like that slow freight."

"I like it, too," said the engineer. "It
has a big job to do."

"Is that your pony?" asked the engineer.
Ginger was running for home.

"Yes," said Randy. "I guess I will have to walk."

"Would you like to ride back with me?" asked the engineer.

"I surely would," said Randy.

Randy climbed up into the nose of the Crimson Rocket.

The train began to move.

"Where is your coal car?" asked Randy.

"I don't use coal."

"What makes the engine go?"

"I burn oil," said the engineer. "The oil makes a motor go. The motor makes electricity. The electricity makes the train go. This is called a Diesel-electric train."

"Boy!" said Randy.

The Rocket came up close to the
slow freight.

Men were working to put the last car
back on the track.

Then Randy walked home.

He sat down and ate his supper with Sue.

Soon he heard the toot-toot of the slow freight as it pulled onto the sidetrack.

Then there was a low too—oot as the Crimson Rocket went on its way.

"What is that whistle?" asked Sue.

"Oh, that is just my new friend, the Diesel-electric," said Randy. "That is a good train, too."

The End